Dear Parents and Teachers,

I SPY A TO Z helps your child learn to read in 4 important steps. The first three steps are achievable by preschoolers. The fourth step, phonics, is achievable by most children at age 6. However, some children achieve it earlier and others at age 7, all within the range of normalcy. The beauty of **I SPY A TO Z** is that there is something here for all children at all ages, even babies and toddlers, who love the sound of rhythm and rhyme.

1. PICTURE CLUES

The first time you read "I spy a baseball," your child will see a picture of a baseball. The second (or third or fourth) time you read "I spy a baseball," pause before saying "baseball." Your child may supply the word for you. That shows that your child is paying attention to picture clues, an important prereading accomplishment.

2. REPETITION CLUES

The first time you read this book, notice that each page begins with the words "I Spy. . ." The second time you read the book, just say "I. . ." and wait. Your child may supply the word "spy." That shows that your child is paying attention to the repetition in the text, another important prereading accomplishment.

3. RHYMING CLUES

The first time you read this book, notice that the lines on each page rhyme. The second time you read the book, pause before saying the last word of line 2. See if your child supplies the word. That shows that your child is paying attention to rhyming sounds and also to picture clues, two prereading accomplishments at the same time!

4. PHONICS CLUES

The first time you read this book, please just enjoy it. Don't jump into phonics unless you know your child is ready. In subsequent readings, notice with your child that certain letters are printed in red. Why? Help your child hear and discover the answer. Your child may notice that not all identical letters are printed in red. Why? Because letters can have different sounds. Such sounds are for later explorations. In this book, we start at the beginning.

The most important teaching tools when teaching reading are patience, the ability to enjoy your child at whatever stage he or she is at, and the desire to share your own love of reading. Your child is always ready to read at some level!

Happy Reading!

Jean Marzollo and Walter Wick

I SPY
A·TO·Z
A BOOK OF
PICTURE
RIDDLES

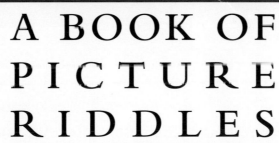

Riddles by Jean Marzollo
Photographs by Walter Wick

Cartwheel
B·O·O·K·S®

SCHOLASTIC INC.
New York   Toronto   London   Auckland   Sydney
Mexico City   New Delhi   Hong Kong   Buenos Aires

I spy a jack , an apple with a bite ,

 a sheriff's badge, and a rabbit that's white.

I spy deer antlers , a thimble hat , three silver snowflakes, and a little white cat.

I spy a basket , a big blue sword ,

two basketballs,  and a pink skateboard.

I spy a baseball , a marble that's blue ,

 a bucket of sand, and a block with a 2.

I spy a cake 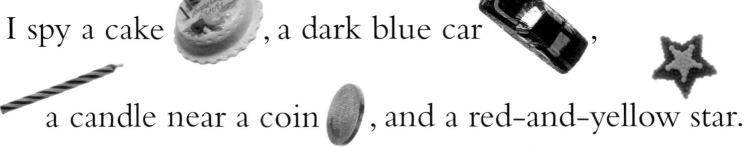, a dark blue car,
a candle near a coin, and a red-and-yellow star.

I spy a clown cap , a circle that's white ,

 a yellow train car,  and a traffic light.

I spy a drum , a red music note ,

 one D on a die,  and an old wooden goat.

I spy a bird's eye  , a doll's round head ,

two D's on a die, and a crayon that's red.

 I spy a belt,  a mask of red,

a necklace of blue, and an elephant's head.

I spy two fish , the face of a cat ,

 a fat red apple, and a firefighter's hat.

I spy a shovel 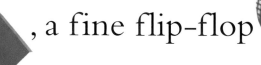 , a fine flip-flop  ,

 a pink flamingo, and a flag on top.

I spy a green bear , a golden star,

a great big arrow, and a cookie guitar.

I spy a penguin 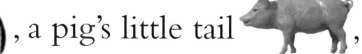, a pig's little tail ,

a big wooden ball, and a girl with a pail.

I spy a heart , blue snake hair ,

horns on a monster, and a happy little bear.

I spy two horses , a card called the Two ,

a yellow hoop, and a hat that's blue.

I spy a pig , a candle's wick,
a blue plane, and a yellow chick.

I spy a traffic sign , a green paper clip,

a bent pin, and a truck for a trip.

I spy jingle bells , a fuzzy bear ,

 a joyful cat, and striped gloves to wear.

I spy a jet , two gold stars ,

 jewels on a crown, and two little cars.

I spy a king , a surfer's hair,

three pink fish, and a koala bear.

I spy a skeleton key, a golden key,

a track for a train, and a yellow golf tee.

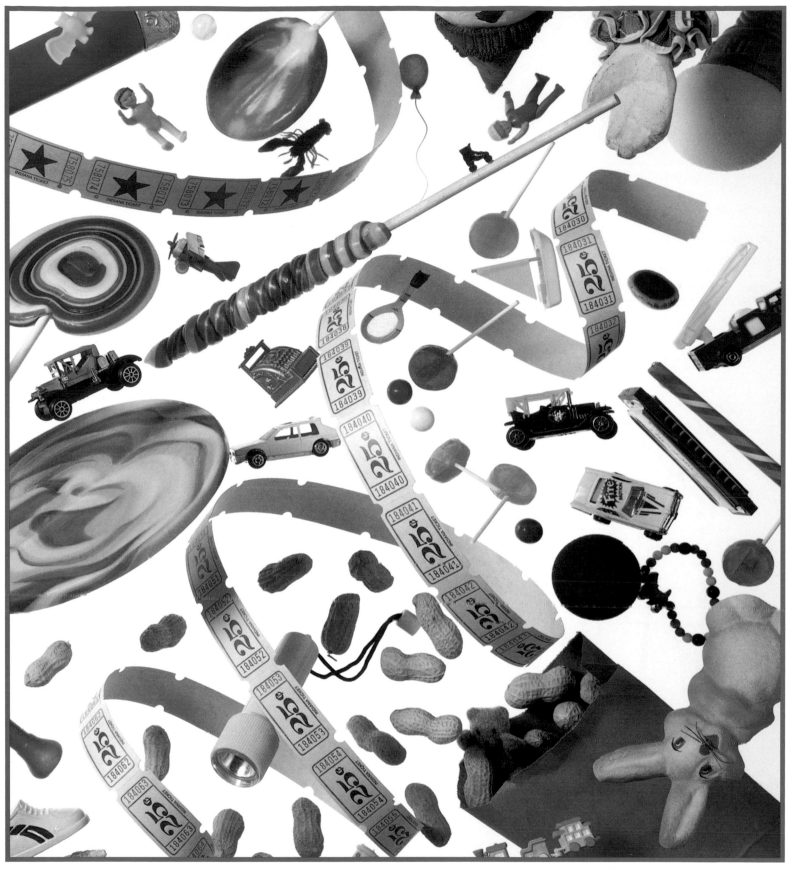

I spy an airplane , a yellow sail ,

 a watermelon,  and a lobster's tail.

I spy a lamp , a dusty old clock ,

 a pair of glasses, and a pig on a block.

I spy a magnet , a man with a bat , a pumpkin's smile, and a small flat hat.

I spy a motorcycle , a nose on a moon ,

a man with a cane,  and a single balloon.

I spy a nickel , a shiny red horn ,

 the man in the moon, and an ear of corn.

I spy a dragon , a little nail ———,

a wooden N, ![person] and a person with a pail.

I spy a helicopter , a flat-head screw,

 two little locks,  and an airplane, too.

I spy a penny , a pencil tip ,

 a spotted cow, and a tiny ship.

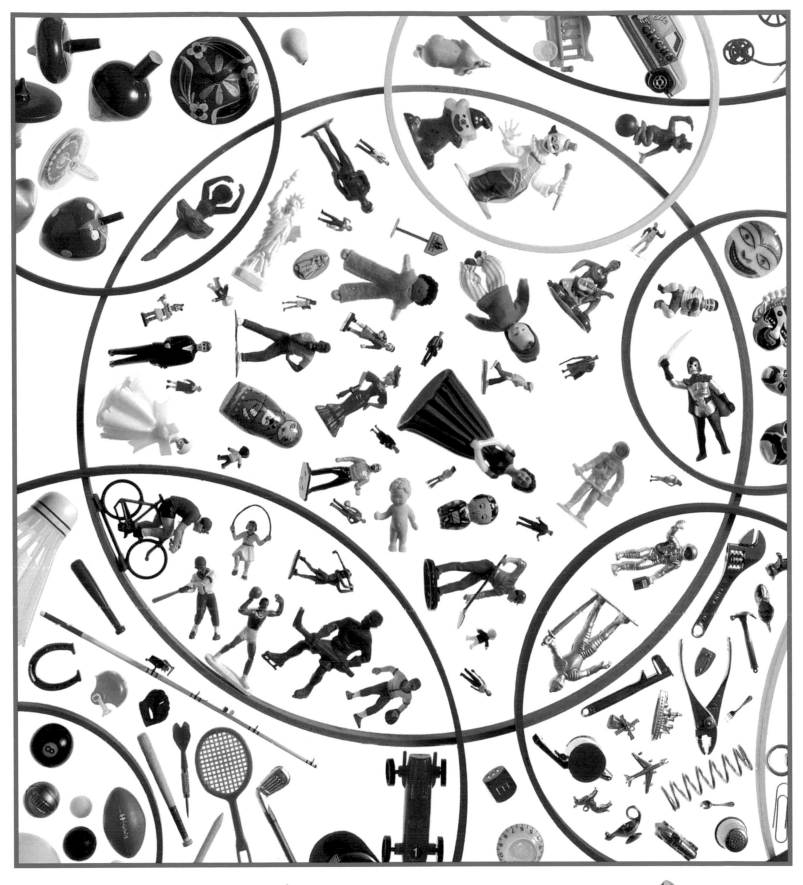

I spy a fishing pole, a purple top, too, a basketball player, and a pear for you.

I spy a queen , a red lunch box ,

 a question mark,  and a quick little fox.

I spy a road sign 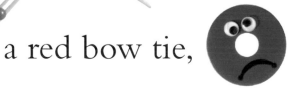, a really red rose,

a red bow tie, and a hole for a nose.

I spy a rubber band , a round ring , a surfer's board,  and a spool of string.

I spy a sailboat , a wide seashell ,

 2 shovels in sand, and a silver bell.

I spy a sailor , a fishing line ,

 a white snowflake, SALTWOOD and a SALTWOOD sign.

I spy a teacup , two tails of a cat ,

 a paper ghost, and a yellow hat.

I spy a puppet's thumbtack knee,

 a red butterfly, and a green palm tree.

I spy two buttons , an orange duck ,

a butterfly , and an empty truck .

I spy an umbrella , WEDNESDAY's sun ,

 big eyelashes,  and a boy on the run.

I spy an evergreen tree , a clean van ,

 the word "MOVIE," and a policeman.

I spy a seven card , a yellow V ,

 a green clover, a block with a 3!

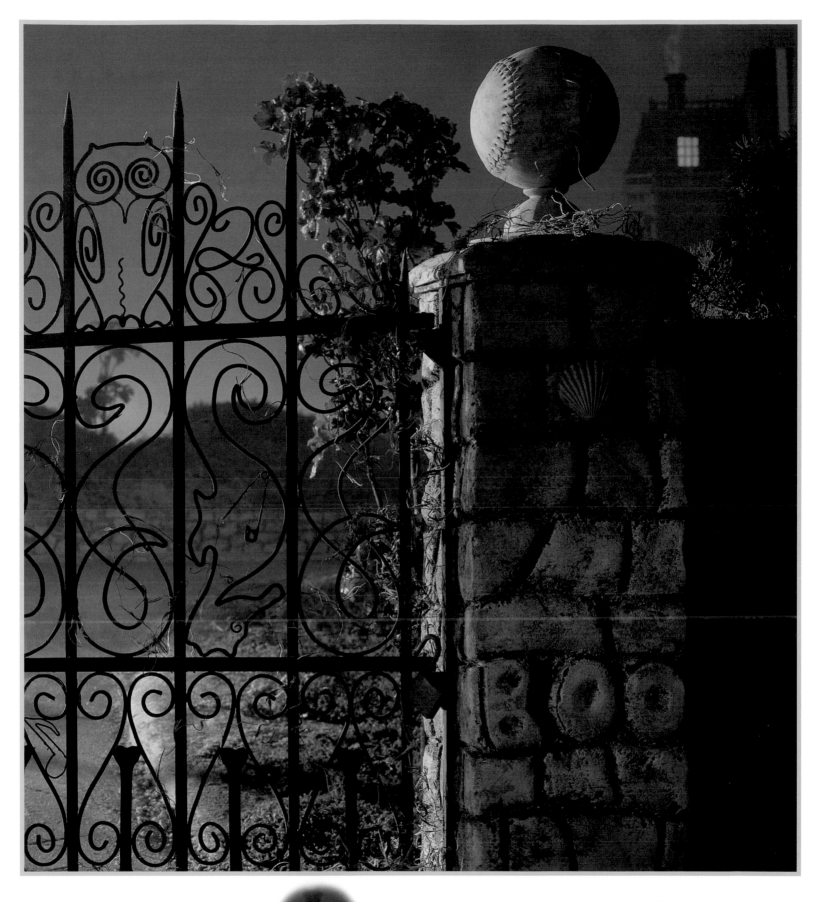

I spy a window , a word on a wall ,

a wire 2 , and an old baseball .

I spy a waterfall , a wooden bat ,

 a wild moose, and a man with a hat.

I spy 5 X's , a small horseshoe ,

6 the number six,  and 3 smiles for you.

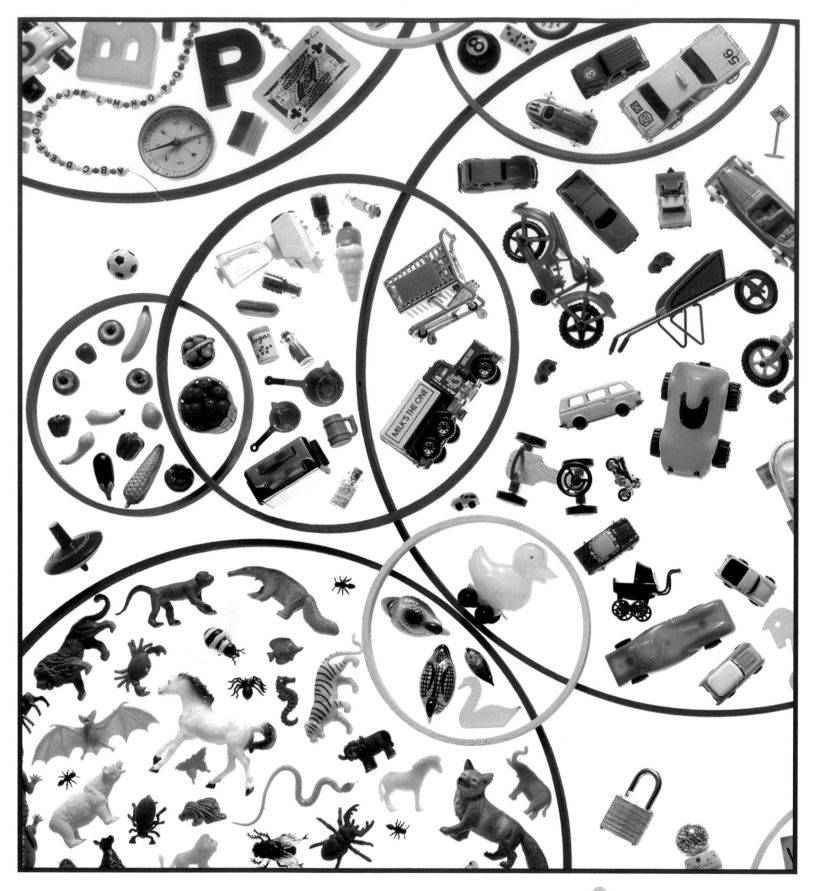

I spy a yellow van , a jack ,

 a yellow duck,  and a little yak.

I spy a zebra , a zebra Z ,

a zebra truck, and a shell from the sea.

Grateful thanks to reading expert Francie Alexander,
Dan Marzollo, and Dave Marzollo for helping with this book.
—J.M. and W.W.

Text copyright © 2007 by Jean Marzollo.
Photo compilation © 2007 by Walter Wick.
Introduction copyright © 2009 by Jean Marzollo.

"Winter Wonderland," "Baking Cookies," "Stocking Stuffers," "Winter Sports," and "Ornaments" from *I Spy Christmas* © 1992 by Walter Wick; "Cubbies," "Arts & Crafts," "Make Believe," "At the Beach," "Blocks," "Tiny Toys," "Odds & Ends," and "Silhouettes" from *I Spy* © 1992 by Walter Wick; "The Hidden Clue" and "The Toy Box Solution" from *I Spy Mystery* © 1993 by Walter Wick; "Peanuts and Popcorn," "The Laughing Clown," and "On the Boardwalk" from *I Spy Fun House* © 1993 by Walter Wick; "Sweet Dreams," "City Blocks," "Monster Workshop," "Flight of Fancy," "Yikes!," and "The Rainbow Express" from *I Spy Fantasy* © 1994 by Walter Wick; "A Is for...," "Levers, Ramps, and Pulleys," "Sorting and Classifying," "Patterns and Paint," "Chalkboard Fun," "Mapping," and "1, 2, 3..." from *I Spy School Days* © 1995 by Walter Wick; "A Secret Cupboard," "Good Morning," and "Creaky Gate" from *I Spy Spooky Night* © 1996 by Walter Wick; "The Treasure Chest Store" from *I Spy Treasure Hunt* © 1999 by Walter Wick. All published by Scholastic Inc.

All rights reserved. Published by Scholastic Inc.
SCHOLASTIC, CARTWHEEL BOOKS, and associated logos are trademarks and/or registered trademarks of Scholastic Inc.

ISBN-13: 978-0-545-10782-2
ISBN-10: 0-545-10782-2

10 9 8 7 6 5 4 3 2 1   9 10 11 12 13

Printed in Singapore
This edition first printing, June 2009